# Trying To Be So Quiet
# &
# Other Hauntings

James Everington

# Praise for James Everington

SINISTER
HORROR
COMPANY

PRESENTS

# TRYING TO BE SO QUIET

## & OTHER HAUNTINGS

### JAMES EVERINGTON

**Trying To Be So Quiet & Other Hauntings**

Edited by J. R. Park
Interior design by J. R. Park
Cover design by Vincent Hunt

**Published by the Sinister Horror Company**

TRYING TO BE SO QUIET & OTHER HAUNTINGS -- 1st ed.
ISBN 978-1-912578-11-5

# ACKNOWLEDGEMENTS

Big thanks to all the people in the UK horror fiction scene who over the last few years have made me so welcome/jealous/took the piss out of me for that review. There's too many to list them all here, but I can't not mention Jim McLeod (I honestly did lose that T-shirt), Dan Howarth (co-editor extraordinaire), Tracy Fahey, Priya Sharma, Simon Bestwick, Cate Gardner, Georgina Bruce, Penny Jones (I hope you paid for this one!), Jay Eales, Timothy Jarvis, Linda Nagle, Steve Shaw, Alison Littlewood, Ray Cluley, Dion Winton-Pollack and Lisa Childs.

And of course my fellow 'Crusties' (Don't ask. Honestly, I don't even really know): Mark West, Phil Sloman, Steve Byrne, Ross Warren and Stephen Bacon

To all the above: I owe you a drink.
Anyone I've forgotten: I owe you two.

And extra special thanks to two people without whom Trying To Be So Quiet wouldn't exist at all: Alex Davis for taking a chance on it the first time round, and Justin Park for enabling this glorious return.

*The stories here are as much about love as loss, and so this book is dedicated to those I love: to my family and friends; to Sarah and Alice.*

# Contents

Trying To Be So Quiet    Pg 01

The Second Wish    Pg 55

Damage    Pg 81

# Trying To Be So Quiet

He packs hastily, not out of fear but indifference. Numbness.

He takes an old shirt from the wardrobe and turns to the open suitcase on the bed; he imagines Lizzie telling him it is the wrong colour, the wrong fit. Her faint smile before she told him. He flings the shirt into the suitcase anyway. His legs are shaking, or the floor beneath him is. When he goes into the bathroom to collect his toiletries, he can't help but glance at the smashed mirror; in the teeth-like pieces of glass that still cling to the frame he sees fragments of movement. Something pretending to be behind him that can't possibly be there.

It doesn't matter, he tells himself. The ghost – he

doesn't believe in ghosts but has no other word for it – is just one more thing that doesn't matter in his dead and paper-thin life.

He goes downstairs and leaves the suitcase by the front door. His train is first thing in the morning.

He pours himself a drink, takes it into the lounge where he turns on the TV. Wearily he notices it is just seven o'clock. The night is still ahead.

Behind him there is a sound, like the house has shifted slightly and is groaning in pro-test.

He turns the TV up.

It doesn't matter, he thinks again. There is no need to start believing in souls now, when he no longer believes in anything else. Lizzie is gone; nothing is haunting him. She'd already been gone on the day of the funeral; whatever had been buried in the rain had no longer been her…

He squirms, as if to avoid the memories.

\*     \*     \*

He remembers the scene from outside, centred on him: stood with his head bowed so that the nape of his neck was exposed to the rain. He hadn't looked at the other mourners, Lizzie's friends and family; instead he had looked down as the spring rain churned up the earth. He remembered a line from

The Waste Land but it was a blank association, passing through his head with no emotional or even intellectual significance. All day words had failed to connect. People had said things like 'we're so sorry,' or 'at least she's not in pain anymore' or 'she's in a better place' and he'd struggled to understand why they were talking. Lizzie's death had sucked not the life out of the world, but the meaning. As he watched the soil being pounded by the beating rain he wondered if what he was feeling was grief. It didn't feel like grief. It didn't feel like anything.

The day they buried her was the first day Lizzie's death seemed real.

They had married in their late twenties, seven years before, moving into a house they had designed and built themselves. Their life together, similarly designed and planned. No children – they'd been saving up. Then came the illness, unexpected and unexplained. Lizzie had been defiant: 'I'm a fighter, aren't I?' And it was true, Lizzie had always been a fighter, an arguer against those things which were unreasonable or unfair. But that hadn't mattered. Nothing had mattered, nothing had worked: not her fighting, not medicine, not his prayers. He'd prayed for the first time in his life, really prayed, like a man alone at sea sending out the words 'help me' on every channel and hearing nothing but static back.

Her dying had been drawn out, her fight just prolonging the pain of her defeat. But still, her actual death had left him dizzy and blank-eyed with shock. Waiting to bury her, his mind had been full of images of earthquakes, of towers and cathedrals falling in silence.

Afterwards it was as if the funeral rain had washed such thoughts away, for his mind was clear and emptiness seemed the only thing left.

When he returned home from the funeral he went into the front room, staring blankly around like it was an anonymous hotel room he had entered for the first time. He remembered he had been crying when he left this room, but already such an idea seemed distant to him. All the objects that had made him weep now seemed meaningless: Lizzie's diary, her mobile phone still with credit, the hairbrush entangled with one of the last hairs her illness had left her. They were things she had touched, but so what? She was gone and nothing she had touched retained any trace of her. He picked up the phone absently. For a moment an image crossed his mind, that of a grief-stricken husband hurling the phone against the wall with a cry – but all he did was place it back down again.

On the wall he was facing hung a picture, of him and Lizzie smiling. He had no idea why they were smiling. They were sitting on a park bench, with the cream stone of old buildings behind them. Oxford. He wondered if even then, as Lizzie had smiled for that picture, the illness had already been within her, biding its time before starting to obliterate everything from the inside outward. Looking away, he felt as if he had some illness, for his emptiness felt heavy in his guts, like some kind of growth or tumour. He moved around slowly because of this, and nothing he saw sparked off much reaction within.

When he got hungry he ate whatever he found in the cupboard.

When he felt thirsty he drank.

When it got dark, he went to bed.

*   *   *

He awoke into the pitch blackness, into a quiet night. His thoughts were still dreamlike and he would have gone straight back to sleep without even remembering that he'd woken, if it hadn't been for an odd sensation that brought him further into consciousness. He could feel someone tapping against his leg.

His first thought was that it was his pulse, throbbing regularly through a vein that he could temporarily sense. Then it felt like fingers, and half-dreaming he smiled with the thought of Lizzie touching his thigh as they slept. Whenever he got into bed before her she would al-ways do things like this, press a cold hand to his chest or cold feet to his, wanting him to warm her. He'd flinch away laughing and she'd say that he wasn't a tactile person...

He sat bolt upright and fumbled for the bedside lamp. Even before he had turned it on the tapping sensation had stopped. He blinked in the sudden light, looking around the room, feeling just how empty it was without her. The only movement was his blurred reflection casting about in confusion in the bedroom mirror. His heart rate sagged back to its earlier speed.

He tried to remember – had it really felt like touch? Really? He could picture Lizzie's hand, pale and slim, and how she used to touch him for reassurance. But most likely it had been merely a dreaming reaction to the rhythms of his own body. You're not a tactile person, you're more visual, he thought, carefully as if the remembered words might bring pain, but there was none to be had. Whatever dream had lingered here tonight couldn't hurt him. It would be best not to think about it. The image of rain mixing up the soil passed briefly through his mind again, and then he got up because he didn't even feel tired anymore.

\*     \*     \*

In the days after the funeral he didn't leave the house and he started to have blackouts, brief lapses of consciousness from which he'd return to the same sleepwalking life he had left. Such brief tumbles into nothingness didn't scare him. Was he sick too? He tried not to think about it. Nevertheless, when he blinked and came to he always had the feeling that something was different about the house than before. Something moved, or toppled over, or askew. But he could never spot what the difference was, and despite himself this nagged at him.

He'd been offered as much compassionate leave as he needed, but the third day after the funeral this nagging drove him back to work.

At the office nothing had changed in his absence, apart from a new woman who had taken the place of one of his colleagues who had retired. He was aware she kept glancing at him, and when he looked back she would fumble clumsily at whatever she was doing. She had obviously been told about him, about Lizzie. He thought about telling her it didn't matter, her curiosity didn't offend him, but he didn't even get up to introduce himself to her.

He worked late, saw everyone glance at him as

they left, the new girl included.

'What the hell are you still doing here?' Peter, his boss, said to him. He glanced at Peter, then back at the figures on his screen. As if where he was mattered. He pressed some keys and the computer displayed the total for each column of figures. It was a meaningless act, but one that filled the time. In a vague way he thought it awful that time still passed even though there was no use or point to it anymore.

'C'mon!' said Peter. 'You can't... no one expected you to be in today, not after... And it's nearly six! Go home. Go and see friends, go for a drink. Go... I don't know.' Peter made a vague gesture with his hands and cast about him. 'Or do you want to come for a drink with me? Shit day so I was going to have one anyway. Take your mind off... things?'

He looked at Peter, and nodded. It seemed as easy as anything else. His only aim now was to avoid irritation. Work did that; he had to do it right otherwise people would bother him. But now Peter was insisting he stopped and okay, he would. He felt like an organism with only a few basic urges, to eat and shit and avoid irritation. Like he was living in a shell, which the world occasionally tapped against the outside of. Not that it could break in, but he might as well stop that tapping.

'It's to find some kind of stability, isn't it?' Peter

said later, drunkenly. 'To come to a place that doesn't change no matter what. Where you can predict your day.'

Amazing he thought, people are still trying to find meaning in what I do. Psychology. He couldn't even find the energy to think the word contemptuously.

\*     \*     \*

He and Lizzie had met while studying at Oxford. They had both been members of the photography society for a while, before giving up. On Sundays trips were arranged to take photographs of the university colleges and gardens. Such buildings had a different meaning to them, studying at the ex-Polytechnic up the hill rather than being students who actually lived within them. To him, it was like a different world, but only if he focused in the right place. He could see the tall spires and gargoyle faces, the wakes of punts and willow tips touching the water – but if he looked left or right, too far, he could see the college merchandise shops, the tourists, the litter from the burger bars.

Afterwards, out of the darkroom, they would look at their pictures of the colleges and compare them to the reality.

'Why did they build them?' he said the second time

they met. 'The college buildings? Didn't they take more than a lifetime to build? Like the cathedrals? So that the people who planned them never saw them finished... That's baffling.' He didn't know whether this was actually true, but he was talking to a girl and it felt like an interesting thing to say.

She smiled at him, raised her eyebrows. 'Who knows why? I guess it's just something you can't explain,' and her answer, meaningless as it was, made him feel dumb and he looked again at the photo of Trinity College in his hands. He imagined he was seeing it more clearly than its designer ever had. He had watched the picture emerge in the darkness of the developing room, something he had called to life against the odds. But was it actually a good photo? He had no idea. He looked up at the small student room he was in, flickering in the light of the candles Lizzie had lit, and back to his photo.

'I don't think I'm cut out for this kind of thing,' he said.

Lizzie was sat quietly, chewing her lip. He had initially thought her plain, but already he was staring to realise how much he liked her. Each time he looked up from one of their photographs he saw one more thing to like: the cut of her brown hair, the faint freckles, the curve of her small breasts. He already suspected she was more intelligent than him.

'What do you study?' he said.

'Anthropology.'

'What is that, exactly?'

She shrugged and smiled. 'Study of everything.' He liked the way she said that. 'So what do you study?'

'Accountancy.'

'Ah, making the numbers add up.' He'd smiled then too, and forgotten about the flat-ness of his photographs.

\*   \*   \*

He dithers by the front door, looking at his suitcase. It is a long wait until the morning train. He could just drive, leave the house and its spooks this very moment, but he is not sure he trusts himself behind the wheel. Besides, getting the train in the morning means he can have a whisky tonight. Another whisky. But still…

If you leave now, he thinks, you are scared after all. Underneath.

And so he doesn't.

\*   \*   \*

He had yet to think the word 'ghost', yet to suspect the supernatural. His blackouts held no significance to him, and he had put the touch he felt in the night out of mind, sure it was nothing more than his imagination. Nor did he initially think that the cracks that had started appearing in the walls of the house were anything more than the usual wear and tear. He knelt by the largest in the bathroom; the cracks branched away from each other like a family tree or crazed writing; they were too slim to put a finger in but for some reason he thought they were deep, boring into the house.

He stood, telling himself the cracks were meaningless for all they looked like writing. Everything was meaningless, now. His joints made a noise as he stood; the aches and twinges of his body seemed far away from his slow thoughts. He looked at his face in the mirror as if it were someone else's composition. His hair was short but still untidy, his forehead pronounced, his cheekbones well-defined with no fat to distort them. He thought his face looked very two-dimensional, like the worst of his old photos of the spires, in which the buildings looked like fakes propped up with wood from behind. He didn't know what was propping him up, or why he shouldn't just fall. His eyes looked like two flat ovals.

Behind him was the equally flat reflection of his bathroom, sparkling and newly-cleaned like it was a bathroom display in a store and not part of someone's actual life. He turned and ducked slightly, so the reflection showed the cracks in the wall directly behind – still without meaning. Not mirror-writing then, he thought, annoyed at himself. When he straightened he did so too fast, and his vision wavered for a second. He blinked, reached to the sink to steady himself.

And in the mirror he saw a face behind him, blurred and ambiguous, moving quickly away to the left.

He started back away from the mirror, feeling his heart quicken. He turned around but there was nothing behind him; the room was quiet and still and the sharp-edged reality of it seemed to leave no room for blurred and ghostly visions.

And how could he be sure what he had seen, when it had been behind him, and a re-flection, and his eyes had been watering anyway? After all, he had seen nothing exact. Just a vague, sexless, nondescript face – no, not even a face. It had been face-shaped but without feature. It must have been just a trick, a trick of the light. Nothing really there.

He thought deliberately of the funeral, and of the water beating into the earth, pointless.

\*   \*   \*

Still, the next day he could not stop thinking of the ghost – he didn't know what else to call the silent, featureless face he had seen, even though the word didn't feel quite right. His apathy was still there, a screen between himself and the world. Everything he observed, or did, or said, seemed to happen on the other side of a pane of glass. But the ghost seemed to flit around on his side, a nagging thought he couldn't rid himself of. He constantly pictured the blank face he had seen in the mirror. Just an empty oval, like something that needed engraving? Or maybe it was something blank from being erased. It suited him to believe the latter. For wasn't Lizzie erased, gone? And wasn't that really the state of the whole world, something blank that had once held meaning?

He wondered if his blackouts were somehow connected, although he couldn't see how. They didn't really disturb him, even if they were signs of illness. They never seemed to happen at the office, or when people were around him, as if he still had some kind of social self that wanted control. And indeed throughout each day he smiled and nodded and tutted in the right places. Anything for a quiet life. Everyone seemed to think he had taken the strain of Lizzie's death well. Occasionally someone would say her name without thinking, or accidentally use the word 'dead' in everyday conversation; and then they would cringe or glance at him quickly, to see how he'd react.

He didn't react. It didn't matter. The words were stones dropped down a well so deep no noise could be heard. 'Lizzie' – so what? She was dead. He thought for the first time in years of the pointless lives of the university builders whose plans they had never lived to see through to fruition (he was forgetting that he might have made this up, to impress a girl). And he thought, that's what everyone is like, because nothingness comes in the end, and it didn't matter if your plans were completed or not, or if you had passed them onto anyone else, or if anyone loved you or whatever. It didn't matter. It didn't matter what he did from now on, for soon he would be nothing, like Lizzie.

It didn't matter if he came into work or not. True, he was there at the moment, he had been every day, but he could not have been. He thought of Peter's words of explanation – 'it's to find some kind of stability, isn't it?' – and he thought it rubbish. He didn't care where he was; why care?

He kept glancing at the new woman who had joined the office in his absence; it was like when he blacked out and awoke sure something had changed – here he knew what the difference was. She had noticed his looks and occasionally smiled back, misinterpreting. It annoyed him, as did the fact that occasionally the sight of her tight skirt gave him an erection. His body still insisted its old lusts and urges were significant. Another thing trying to claim his attention on his side of the pane of glass. He tried to think nothing but a cold anger towards the new girl (whose name was Marie); I could fuck you or not fuck you, he thought, rape you or not rape you, and it just wouldn't matter. Wouldn't matter if we cared or not. For sooner or later we'll both be lying dead whilst people cover us over with dirt. He thought back to when he had made love to Lizzie – what had he felt then? Togetherness? Foreverness? But how could that be; what illusions those seemed now.

\*       \*       \*

Half past nine, fourth whisky. He wishes it were morning already, that he was already on the train. His vision is blurry, both from alcohol and from the tears. But what is there to look at, after all? What is there to see, other than the reminders of his life with Lizzie around him? It is preferable blurred.

The figure in the corner of his vision, moving as if trying to attract his attention, is preferable blurred.

\*       \*       \*

He kept seeing the ghost, a vague and ill-defined movement in every reflective surface. Such simple acts as shaving became problematic, as that blank, featureless face kept appearing – hazy and not just due to the steam blurring up the mirror.

He had the uncomfortable feeling that it wasn't quite as featureless as it had been be-fore. Each time he saw it, he couldn't help but think it was imperceptibly different in some way from last time, more nuanced or irregular... He was reminded of the feeling he had when he came to from one of his blackouts, casting around his house convinced that something was changed.

There hadn't been any period of disbelief, of denial – as soon as it became obvious that something supernatural was happening, he'd accepted it as just something else pointless. He had a ghost. Well so what? It didn't matter. He'd not tried to find a rational explanation, for what was 'rational' about a world where people like Lizzie just died? A ghost was no less rational than that; he used the word 'ghost' in his thoughts because there was no other, not be-cause he thought it was Lizzie. Despite the feminine aspect to what might be emerging from its face...

He tried to think of it as 'the ghost' or just as 'it'. Never as 'she'.

*   *   *

Oxford had been a romantic place to fall in love. Fortunately they hadn't lived right in the centre of it. For real life there had been the outskirts, the terraces the same as anywhere else. Here they had lived and studied, partied and been sick, suffered a pregnancy scare, and built their plans for the future. So they weren't deluded romantics, and they knew enough about the real life compromises that made relationships. But they knew the unreal aspects too, and then Oxford seemed perfect. They could walk along the Cherwell holding hands, they could sit in the parks and see the architecture, the almost unreal spires and ghostly white buildings. And, because they were human, they could sneer with inverse snobbery at the 'real' Oxford students, and then laugh at themselves for doing so.

He wasn't quite sure how he had fallen in love. Certainly when he'd first seen Lizzie she hadn't seemed the kind of girl he could go for. But each time he had spoken to her it was like something was being built up; he hadn't consciously tried to seduce her for she was smarter than him and would have seen through it. Her cleverness was something she hid from most people as if it were an embarrassment, but not from him. When she put him right it was always with a smile. Sometimes when he said something, just her silence before she replied was enough to make him realise he was wrong.

'Do you believe in ghosts?' she had said to him one day, looking at him quizzically. He guessed he could understand why someone's mind would turn that way, in this old city with its tall white buildings, the saints and gargoyles carved into them. They had been walking among them all morning and were now resting on a bench in the centre of town before attempting the walk back up the hill.

'No,' he said, after a pause.

'What about Heaven?' she said. 'Or Hell?' He knew her well enough by now not to try and second guess her beliefs; her asking the question didn't signify either way.

'No.'

'You just believe it all stops? That nothing carries on?'

'No.' He smiled as he repeated this, and saw Lizzie's eyebrows lift. Sometimes he could surprise her too.

'You can't say no to both!' she said laughing.

'I said I didn't believe in either. Because I don't know what happens, do you? What do you believe?'

'I believe... I can't believe my brother doesn't still

exist somehow,' Lizzie said quietly, and he realised again how stupid he was. She'd once told him that a few years ago her older brother, who she said was a genius, had been killed in a car accident. He had supposed this was an innocent conversation, but obviously it wasn't.

'Come here,' he said, and hugged her. He felt very protective of her, like there was a whole universe of harm trying to touch her. Over her shoulder he could see the cream walls of one of the colleges; it was as if he could feel the cool stone presence of the building. And if it was true that whoever had planned this had never lived to see it completed he thought that the architect had at least been able to sense it, like he could. Even when he closed his eyes he felt the weight and presence of the building, and what was inside too – he had never been inside but he could picture the cool and gloomy interior. And he held Lizzie even more tightly, not through fear that one day she might be gone, not through fear at all.

\* \* \*

He came to in the hallway. He had no idea how long this latest blackout had lasted: he had been putting on his jacket to go to work, turned to pick up his keys and then – then just nothing, a gap, and he had returned to himself still in the hallway, not sure if the time he had missed was seconds or hours.

He looked around him; there were cracks in the magnolia walls of the hallway, radiating from a central point in lines that looked like illegible handwriting. Could he be sure that they hadn't been there before? The pattern looked like someone had smashed a fist or palm into the wall. And he knew from numb experience that the ghost could interact physically, could touch things. But still, wasn't that thought giving the thing more agency, more significance than it deserved? All of the ghost's acts seemed random and pointless, which confirmed his view that the universe was too. It had cracked his walls, appeared in steamy mirrors and maybe once tried to touch him. Weren't ghosts supposed to give warnings from beyond the grave, or threats or messages? But there was nothing like that. It seemed almost quotidian and if he didn't look too closely he could convince himself that the cracks in the walls were just in the plaster, and not deeper into the material of the house itself.

He arrived to the office slightly late, but still felt annoyed as people merely glanced at him sympathetically. Peter didn't come over and bollock him, no one made wise cracks about his tardiness. He felt a jolt of anger as he looked around – everyone engaged in pointless, even moronic tasks. The analysts frowning at their PC screens, the temps gossiping about performance bonuses around the coffee machine, the salespeople lying at the top of their lungs down the phones. As if any of it mattered! He wanted to rub their faces in how pointless it all was. They were just building their dreary little spires up into the sky.

He noticed that Marie, the new girl, wasn't there, and when Peter stopped by his desk he found himself asking where she was. He told himself it was just to break the uncomfortable silence where there would have previously been small talk; he didn't mind the silence but if he didn't break it Peter would and maybe with something about Lizzie. Nevertheless, when he asked about Marie, Peter still looked uncomfortable.

'Compassionate leave,' he said. 'Her grandmother died. They were very close I think; she's devastated. Still, I imagine you know how that... I mean... you're in the same uh...'

He ignored Peter's discomfort. 'Devastated' – yes that was it. Not in the way Peter meant it, not tears and raging dramatics, but the quiet devastation of a toppled building after the dust had settled and everything had stopped moving.

'We're going to send some flowers,' Peter said, 'if

you want to chip in?' He nodded absently, pulled out some money from his wallet. Money was another thing which had lost all of its previous significance. 'She was an interesting person,' Peter was saying, 'used to be a ballerina, apparently, performed in... I don't know. Then she was an MP, the first female one in her area and...'

'And you think that matters?' he said, not knowing that he was going to interrupt, or with how much passion, until he did so. 'None of that matters.'

Peter looked at him queerly. 'Of course it matters. Now look, I know...'

'None of it matters,' he said again. His words felt like trapped things he hadn't been aware of, rushing to escape. 'The death at the end cancels everything out. Life is like one long sum whose final answer is zero. Yours, mine, Marie's, her grandmother's. It doesn't matter what the other numbers are, it still ends in nothing.'

The silence that stretched out after he'd spoken seemed full of all the possible replies Peter might make.

'Don't go speaking to Marie when she's back,' Peter eventually said, turning away as if to stop himself saying more.

Later, he didn't understand why he had argued. If nothing mattered why should he care if others believed that? The anger in his voice, his exaggerated words, had all argued against him. He had been filled with sudden emotion, as much panic as anger, as if someone had shaken the shell that enclosed him.

He felt calmer by the time he returned home. He looked at the cracks in the hallway again as he took off his jacket, but they never increased in size when he wasn't there.

*     *     *

The weekend came and he could find no reason to go into work. He stayed inside, having nowhere else to go, and he wondered what was going to happen next. He could tell some-thing was coming, some new disturbance. The feeling reminded him of nothing so much as when Lizzie had paused before answering him, her silence letting him realise he was wrong before she told him why. This pause felt the same – it felt like a new thing, to be wondering about the future again, and he didn't like it. In the days since Lizzie's funeral he had lived solely in the present, occasionally looking back at the past with the scornful attitude a teenager had to his childhood. But the future hadn't been worth thinking about, for the future was a brief flurry of days curtailed by death coming hard on their heels. But now, faced with the unexpected in the short-term, he worried. His body, unused to stress, reacted by breaking out into sweats at odd moments, making his heart shake, making him walk into rooms and forget why.

When it came, it almost seemed like an anticlimax – the ghost appeared in the mirror again. It obviously only had a small repertoire of tricks. Its face didn't flit away but hovered be-hind his shoulder this time – he turned around but of course there was nothing visible in the clear-cut world on his side of the mirror. When he turned back its face still hung in the same reflected space. He had been correct that it had gained some kind of definition, some kind of structure: he could see the architecture of its eye sockets, of its cheekbones, underneath its grey and featureless flesh. He laughed aloud when he saw it, the symbolism was so crude – yes, yes, a skull under every face. It was like a Halloween toy held up to scare him. Had he really been waiting uneasily for this? The supernatural world was as trite as the natural one.

The face convulsed, or rather the surface of the glass seemed to. Like he was viewing the face in water rippled by some disturbance, and he had to wait for it to settle to see it clearly again. And when he did it had changed, become more substantial: the eye sockets less empty, the cheekbones softened by a layer of muscle. The mirror seemed to ripple again, and the face was even more defined when it reappeared: as if the ghost had realised that the way to build a face was from the inside outward. There was hair now, and closed eyelids, and the lips of a closed mouth.

'No, no...' he said, but he was unable to step back from the mirror or look away. For each time the ghost's face rippled and changed it was clearer what was being built up: Lizzie's features, Lizzie's face. The eyelids opened and her eyes were shockingly blue; he remembered how her eyes had seemed the last part of her to fade as she died, blazing with life even as such life as was in her dimmed. The eyes seemed to be looking at him, and then he saw the mouth open. The tongue briefly licked its lips. He remembered that habit; every time he saw someone else do it he thought of Lizzie – it meant she was about to speak. And that he was sure he wouldn't be able to stand, to hear if this ghost could reproduce her voice as well as her image.

And then what blurred was not the mirror's surface but his whole vision; his out-stretched arm pulled down the mirror as he fell.

\* \* \*

When he came to he was lying on the bathroom floor covered in glass; he had some small cuts to his face and scalp but nothing serious. He had never fallen whilst being blacked out as far as he knew, and he wondered if it signalled some new, more aggressive phase of the ghost's behaviour. The thing was obviously so dumb that it didn't understand that leaving him staring at Lizzie's face in the mirror would have been more painful than any cuts.

It wasn't Lizzie, he told himself as he pulled himself up by holding on to the sink. Where the mirror had been there were a number of large, deep cracks in the wall – he imagined something malignant hammering its fists against the wall as he had lain there unconscious. He had never seen Lizzie hit anything, never seen her react violently even when they had argued.

Lizzie was dead – that was all he had to remember. Maybe something could use her image, just like he could reproduce a photograph of her, but that didn't mean it was her. He thought of how the face had seemed to gain substance each time. He admitted it, it had been a good trick. But it had just been a trick. He knew that beneath the earth Lizzie's face was going through the reverse process (not that that was really her anymore, either). It was an inevitable process – a continuation really of the process that had killed her. A gradual lessening, a movement towards entropy.

Now, when he felt uneasy, he found such thoughts

oddly comforting.

*     *     *

It had been a quiet night because it wasn't term time, and so the Oxford streets had seemed safe to have a public argument. The few passersby had all been drunk. They had been drunk themselves. That had been part of the problem.

The argument was soon all insults, unoriginal and unmemorable. Whatever they had actually been arguing over was soon lost as they just began attacking each other: you're so smug; you never listen to anything anyone else says; you're sarcastic because you're insecure; you have to have everything spelled out for you; you like seeing others fail because it makes you feel superior; I could get someone better than you.

Eventually they both fell silent, breathing heavily as if they had been physically fighting. They were surrounded on all sides by the college buildings and their stone walls seemed to intensify the coldness of the night. Lizzie was staring at him, her blue eyes wide and unreadable. He staggered a little with the enormity of what he had said, what he thought he had done. He closed his eyes, ashamed at his own self-destructiveness. He suddenly felt sober and like he was going to be sick.

'Well that's that isn't it?' he said, to himself as much as her. 'No going back from that is there?'

'What do you mean?' Lizzie, her voice still harsh as if they were still arguing. He re-plied in kind, for once annoyed at the way she spoke as if he were stupid:

'Us. Us, over. We can't go back after all that's been said, can we?' He spoke fiercely but logically, like he was trying to think his way through some difficult mental arithmetic. He opened his eyes to look at her and was appalled by how beautiful he still found her. Pointlessly so, now. Her skin was very pale in the darkness, seemingly the same colour as the ancient stone behind her. He thought of all the times they had walked beneath these spires and white brick, and wondered how it could all have been cancelled out – all they'd done together, all the times he couldn't even remember.

'Oh you idiot,' she said. 'Do you really think it's all so fragile? That it's all been for nothing?' He was surprised by how fierce her voice was.

Eventually of course they made up, as anyone could have predicted. Everyone said they were in love just to look at them. And the making up was nice, but sometimes they had to work at it, occasionally not saying or doing as they wished to help their relationship, to build it stronger.

*     *     *

The following Monday he was in work early, wanting to get away from the house. Not that the ghost's tricks in the mirror had scared him, not that exactly... he just didn't want to see them again. He knew the ghost was just some vacuous thing, some supernatural trickster copying Lizzie, clumsily reproducing her outward form. But where was it getting its energy from, and why had it picked his wife, and how had it picked her when nothing of her remained? From the past, his mind answered, only from the past. The voice in his head was like another ghost, whispering things right on the edge of hearing when all he wanted was quiet.

He thought he would be the first at the office, but when he arrived Marie was already there. She gave him a slight smile before looking away. He debated whether to go up to her and say he was sorry for her loss, but he remembered how such platitudes had annoyed him at Lizzie's funeral. He doubted he could make it convincing anyway – his own feelings barely troubled him inside of his shell, much less the feelings of others.

And besides, he knew he looked like shit; he'd barely slept all weekend, and had hurriedly dressed that morning. He felt too hot, and his eyes were blurry as he tried to ignore Marie in his peripheral vision and focus on the figures on his PC screen. They made no sense.

The others gradually started to come into the office, and he was aware that each of them made the effort to stop by Marie's desk and talk to her. The usual nonsense. He had heard it all a hundred times at Lizzie's funeral, and it sounded like Marie would hear it a hundred times herself. He wanted to yell at them to just leave her alone.

But he knew this was all a relapse; why should he care if the others bothered Marie? It was all that damn ghost's fault. It had managed to break down a few barriers; he would have to work at rebuilding them. After all, supernatural events had no more claim to significance than any others. But for the moment he did feel tensed up and very tired, all at once. He hoped, at work and away from his house, he would feel the welcome numbness start to creep back.

His screen blackened with the shadow of a face falling over it, and for a moment he thought... But it was just Peter, standing behind him and looking over his shoulder at the report on his screen.

'Go home,' Peter said.

'What? Peter, I'm fine. I...'

'I'm not speaking as your friend this time. I'm saying it as your boss. Whatever you've been doing this morning is all bollocks. Go home – you can't even add up!' Peter waved his hand angrily at the screen. 'Look, I know what you've been through, but you chose to come back to work when you did. Either go home so someone else can write this report, or sort it out.'

'But I...'

'Just don't sit here messing about!'

'Okay!' he said angrily. He was aware the rest of the staff were pretending they couldn't hear, despite the open-plan office. He flushed and when he glanced around involuntarily he saw only Marie was looking at him. But all he could feel was anger and he didn't meet her gaze; instead as Peter walked away he looked back to his screen. Peter was right – it was bollocks. The report was supposed to be for an important client, and he hadn't even managed to put the decimal point in the right place at the end! He set himself to rebuilding the report, frowning in concentration.

It was at least an hour before he asked himself why.

\* \* \*

He has heard of lucid dreams, ones in which the dreamer knew himself to be dreaming, but he has never heard of lucid blackouts before. He feels himself go, his conscious control of his body falling away, but this time his personality remains, a passenger observing his actions from outside. Or has it been like this every time and he just hasn't remembered?

Maybe this time you'll remember enough to know what's changed – he is thinking of the nagging sense of difference he feels after each blackout. He doesn't feel scared, indeed the detachment he feels is like the ideal he has been striving for ever since Lizzie's death. He watches as his body rises from the chair in the front room in which he had gratefully sat with a drink after getting back from work. His body feels numb to him as he walks over to the far side of the room, and he wonders if he would feel pain if his body should stumble or fall. He stops and his head turns towards the pictures of himself and Lizzie on the wall; one in particular of the two of them before some dirty white Oxford building not long after they had first met. He reaches up to touch it as if to straighten it, but with clumsy hands that leave it more askew than before. If he'd been watching such action on a stage he'd have said they looked like the actions of a grieving man, but what explanation could there be here? Is the ghost inside, he wonders, are the blackouts really periods where the ghost ousts me from my own body? But to what end, if so? A ghost that leaves pictures askew – what kind of haunting is that?

He, or whatever is driving, turns suddenly, as if responding to an unexpected noise, although he has heard none. He walks out into the hallway, kneels, and prods at the cracks in the wall a few times (to no purpose that he can see) until the carpet beneath is dusted with loose chips of plaster. Then with another abrupt reaction to something unknown, he turns and goes upstairs, to the little office room they had made the house's smallest bedroom into. He goes straight to one of the dustiest, most crumpled box-files and pulls out some old, cream coloured documents from it. The plans for a house; this house. The house he and Lizzie had always said they 'built' even though they'd done none of the actual labouring.

He hasn't knowingly been into this room since Lizzie's death.

He rifles through the papers and he, the he who is watching, wishes whatever is con-trolling him would stop, because despite the fact that all he can see are simple black and white diagrams, he knows there is great pain here, just straining to reach him on his side of the divide. He feels his head tilt backwards, and feels his mouth open wide as if to scream...

And then there is a screaming, but not from him – the screaming is high and seems to whirl all around him. It seems to fill the entire house and shake it to its foundations, for it is loud, like a thousand people screaming all at once. He is on his feet and turns round as if to identify the source of the sound, but it is everywhere. The scream is without pause or alteration; nothing stops to draw breath. He flees from it, stumbling from the box room and downstairs; he can feel the banister shaking under his hand, or feel his own hand shaking. He isn't sure. Why is it running from its own screaming? he thinks. At the foot of the stairs he assumes he is going to continue to rush forward, out of the front door and away from this shrieking house, but in-stead he watches as he turns left and dashes back into the front room.

Into silence.

The screaming has stopped and he looks around the room, searching for anything out of place. But he can see nothing. Is this where he wakes? But that doesn't happen and as he looks at the room he is aware that his senses seem unnaturally sharp; he feels aware of every item in the room, of the dust on the TV screen, of the marks on the wall he hasn't noticed before. Of the whorls of the pattern in the carpet and of the faded safety sticker still attached to the plug of the lamp. He is aware of a faint draft from the window, and of the faint hum of electrical equipment on standby, and of the smell of old magazines and books on the shelves, which themselves smell of varnish.

And then, without warning, he is aware of Lizzie standing in the centre of the room.

He doesn't react at all, for whilst he is still not in control of his body, it doesn't seem like anything else is anymore either. He just stands and stares at Lizzie – it is not some spectral re-production of her, but her whole and alive. He takes her in, the familiar contours of her body and face, the angle of her cheekbones, the curve of her belly. He cannot read the expression in her eyes, and he has the impression – so familiar! – that here is something she wishes him to understand, some message which he is too thick to comprehend first time.

He is as hyper-sensitively aware of Lizzie as he is of the room: he can hear her heart beat, sense the expansion and contraction of her lungs and the gape of her arteries as blood rushes through them. The minute growth of her hair. He can sense the air temperature in the room increase and her pores open slightly in response. He can smell her from across the room. But also –

All his defences are down and he wants to cry out, because also in Lizzie he can sense the illness that will kill her. He can feel it, a black and slug-like tumour, expanding, spreading poison through her veins, polluting the heart of every cell. Beneath all the life in her he can sense the death. And not just in Lizzie, but all around – he can feel the cells in him die and not be replaced, feel the way the walls of his house are starting to fracture, feel the sun start to lose its heat and the universe's forward rush start to slow... Feels eternity as a brief explosion, struggling for a second or two, before blackening to nothing.

He looks at Lizzie again and it is too much, despite not being fully present in his body the grief is too much, and this time it is a conscious act as he shields himself behind a wall of apathy. His precious barriers and screens.

She turns away from him. She was always smarter than he was.

The screaming starts again, and he physically hides himself against it, cradling his head in his hands and crouching down. It is a female scream he knows now; of course it is Lizzie's scream. It is her scream of futile protest at the moment of death, the scream she was denied by the drugs and machines plugged into her. Her death scream, extended and given life...

When he comes to this time, he knows what has

changed. He is crying, and his throat is raw.

\*     \*     \*

He could barely focus his eyes at work the next day. The office around him was fuzzy and lacked clarity. People came and spoke to him and after a few seconds their words receded to a distant buzz, their faces became mere background. He had no idea what he was replying to them. But the idea of going home instead threatened to bring down his defences and lead to panic. His house, the haunted house – it made sense, he supposed, where else would a ghost live but where they'd died? Of course, Lizzie hadn't really died at home, but doped up and un-responsive at hospital, yet it still seemed to him that it was logical – she would come back to the place where they'd planned their lives together, until the disease. Not that he believed the thing was in any way Lizzie of course. It belonged to the world after the rain had soaked the grave-yard earth, to the world that held no meaning. He just needed to get back to that world himself, to get a few quiet days away from the spook and its clever impressions of life and significance.

He got up from his desk and walked across the office; the distance he crossed seemed a thousand miles. People were looking at him but their looks barely registered. Peter looked up as he approached and his eyes widened – he wondered how he looked to Peter's eyes? Drunk? He couldn't even guarantee that he wasn't; if he couldn't trust his memories because of the black-outs how did he know he hadn't drunk bottle after bottle? But lack of memory was better than what he had seen during the last blackout.

'How are you?' Peter said. 'You look... well, not so good. How is that report coming along?'

'Not so well. Not at all – you'll have to give it to someone else. Peter, can I have the rest of the week off? I know it's short notice but...'

'Yes, no problem,' Peter said, too quickly.

He felt he should offer some explanation. 'I'm going away for a few days,' he said, 'to get away from... the house. The memories, you know...'

'Yes good idea,' Peter said, cutting him off. He looked uncomfortable. 'Where to?'

'Oxford.' He hadn't even realised himself until he said it out loud.

Neither of them knew what to say next.

He stepped back from Peter's desk, and then started as he heard a scream behind him. Marie's yelp quickly turned into an embarrassed laugh, and she was still smiling as she bent to pick up the documents he'd inadvertently caused her to drop. He didn't have the wit to stoop to help her until she was almost done, and as he knelt she met his eyes with a look he saw was concerned for him. He clumsily handed her one of the files back, and she thanked him. Looking at her face he suddenly understood why he considered her attractive. She had brown hair cut short, and faint freckles. She licked her lips as though about to say something else to him and he quickly hurried away from her, having to put a hand to the wall to steady himself. Lizzie's ghost faces were everywhere.

\*　　\*　　\*

That had been today. Or rather, yesterday – it has just turned midnight. He drains the last of his whisky, feeling numb and light-headed. No dreams for him tonight, the drink will see to that, and by this time tomorrow he will be in another city where the housebound ghost can-not follow. Maybe it will have faded entirely by the time he returns – he has learned everything fades. Slowly he climbs the stairs to the bedroom; there are cracks all up its length now. Oxford, he thinks; he hasn't been there since he and Lizzie were married. Surely it can't be the place of white stone spires and college parks that he remembers? His memory of Oxford seems improbable; everything he remembers happening there has an unrealistic backdrop. Every memory with Lizzie a blurred and out of focus photograph.

*    *    *

The train is warm and its carriages sway rhythmically and he sleeps. There are no dreams and when he wakes he feels more refreshed than he has done for weeks. He realises he has been woken by the cessation of noise and motion; the train has come to a halt in the middle of nowhere. There is a collective groan; he groans too. An unapologetic voice apologises over the speakers. The passengers stir and look at each other as if they too had all just woken. Their collective lack of influence over the situation seems to form a temporary bond between the solitary travellers, and the previously quiet carriage fills with noise of chatter, as people tell each other where they are going, and who to see.

'To Oxford,' he replies grudgingly to the man opposite. 'It's where I met my wife.' The old man offers him a cup of coffee from his thermos, and he has to admit he enjoys it. The man is going further than him, all the way to the south coast where he is part of some activist group which cleans beaches. He tries to look interested as he drinks the man's coffee, but he is grateful when the train finally moves again and everyone falls silent, their shared misfortune over. Pointless, he reminds himself, pointless, pointless, in time to the train's rhythm.

He is surprised by how little Oxford seems to have changed. He walks from the station towards the centre, where he looks around like a tourist. The shops and billboards at ground level have all altered, but the white stone college buildings remain unchanged. It is hard to re-member that they were once not here, that they were planned and built deliberately.

And one day they won't be here again, he thinks sourly. His tiredness is returning and the tolerance he had felt to other people on the train has been replaced by dislike of the crowd of tourists pushing and gawping around him. He dislikes their peering faces and constant at-tempts to capture the university architecture on cheap camera phones. Pictures used to be for looking at; now the mere act of taking them seems enough. The noise of their chatter drowns out his own thoughts, and when he recalls that the crowded street he is standing in is the one where he and Lizzie had their first argument he is glad for that. Why has he come here anyway – for memories? He shakes his head, annoyed with himself. Memories are as pointless as every-thing else.

He heads away from the crowds and tourist buses

and towards one of the parks near Trinity College. He sets to walking around it, his head bowed. Here at least he can get some solitude, for the park seems deserted. He is starting to think this whole trip is a mistake; why has he come back to this city of old dreams? To flee a ghost? But why flee – it is just a reminder of death and he can't flee those. The fallen leaves under his feet are as much a symbol of death as some poor, spectral reproduction of Lizzie's form. So what if it is causing him black-outs and shaking the walls of his house until they crack? So what if it screams; these last few months he has felt like doing that himself.

He has learned the lesson of ghosts. He thinks again of the funeral. Both the tears of Lizzie's friends and the dignified silence of her parents seemed like improper attitudes. Because both reactions assumed that things still mattered. As if Lizzie's actions and personality alive could compensate for her death; as if theirs now could make up for their own... –

these thoughts come to his head automatically when he has nothing else to think of, like lyrics to an old song. The rain and wet earth.

Around the corner, comes Lizzie.

Her gait, the way her hands are shoved into her pockets to keep them warm – all this he sees with a thrill of recognition. His mind reels with love, for that first moment he can't process the fact that this is just the ghost, just a ghost, not Lizzie herself, for ghosts are meant to be translucent things appearing in the corner of the eye, and not just to come casually strolling round the corner of an Oxford park.

She pauses about six feet away from him; he can see the depression of footsteps behind her in the damp leaves. It is a hateful trick of the ghost, he thinks, to copy so exactly the woman he loves. The one strange aberration is her clothing, for he has never seen Lizzie wear such an overcoat before, long and cream white. What did the thing want from him? He longs to go and hold her, the effect is so lifelike. He wonders which would be worse if he did – touching nothing or touching warm skin.

The ghost is smiling, the faint smile of knowing something he doesn't. But it is a kind smile too, as if saying he would know, someday. Her normally pale skin is red, as if with the cold, and he realises he hasn't seen her look this healthy for over a year, since the illness had really taken hold. Under the mysterious new coat he can see the rise and fall of her breasts; her eyes are bright and he can see her breath, visible in the autumn air. It is hard to picture such a person getting ill, never mind wasting away to nothing. Her death seems a terrible affront.

But he must remember that this thing isn't Lizzie.

Whatever is due to happen here, whatever confrontation is coming, he would do well to remember that.

He looks around but there is no one else here to see what he is seeing. The only thing moving amid the fallen leaves and bare trees is a squirrel burying nuts, rationing for the real cold. Its eyes are very dark and it watches him every time he moves, but whether it is aware of the silent ghost or not he can't tell. Aren't animals supposed to be sensitive to the supernatural? He can see above the trees the white sky and the white spires reaching into it. Because they are the same colour as the sky the spires seem hazy, dream-like.

The ghost is still looking at him, still smiling the same faint smile and waiting for him to react.

What is it doing here? A ghost was surely meant to stay put in the place it haunted. But he thinks that here, this place, is one he remembers. He has been here before, this exact spot, with Lizzie. What had happened here? He can't quite remember.

The ghost starts to move towards him and he warily takes a step back in case it means to touch him, but it just walks around him, circling, smiling at him all the time. He turns, clumsily, to keep her in view.

'What?' he says. 'What?'

Her eyes leave his for just a moment, and look

towards the university buildings. He looks too. He remembers how they had looked together once, first through the two-dimensional eyes of a camera, then just looking. Not even really that, for who looks at buildings they see every day? But maybe they had been aware, throughout their courtship, of the presence of the old, solid, cream-coloured buildings. He can feel her eyes on him, watching his reaction. He remembers how Lizzie used to say things, to see how he reacted.

'But they're not timeless,' he says, 'that's the point.' It's as if a conversation has re-started mid-flow. But if that's true, then he must be supplying both sets of lines, for the ghost hasn't spoken. Something within shifts, he can almost feel it, and his voice becomes more strident, like when he used to argue with Lizzie. 'You're not lasting either,' he says, 'whatever you are! That's the whole fucking point. You're dead, you're not Lizzie, Lizzie's gone.'

The ghost pauses in its circling him; the sound of her footsteps in the leaves ceases. She just smiles. There is no countering his clichés with clichés of her own.

'Gone!' he says again. 'Rotting away, just like I am, like all this…' She circles him again; he has to turn more and more quickly to keep her in sight. He feels dizzy and for a second his vision fogs, as if he is going to pass out. He stumbles. For some reason this makes him furious. He realises he has been very angry since Lizzie's death, angry at the fucked up state of the universe. 'Are you trying to tell me there's some point behind all this?' he yells. He flings wide his arms to encompass the trees and park and the buildings beyond…

And then he feels, as he flings his rage out into the open space of the park, something tumble inside of him. The grief that has been inside all along feels suddenly exposed, unprotected, and he cries out loud.

The silence that stretches out afterwards feels full of all the possible things she might say, but doesn't. Doesn't have to, for he knows her so well. He feels again the tired sobriety he felt when he and Lizzie had argued in the Oxford streets.

He looks again at the ghost, wrapped in a strange coat that Lizzie never wore. It must be a deliberate mistake, for everything else is copied so perfectly. But why make a deliberate error in translation, when without it the replication would seem the perfect thing? Nevertheless he is glad the ghost has done this – without the discrepancy, he might have believed it her and broken down to sob in the fallen leaves. His head is full of memories of Lizzie alive, memories that don't just seem to induce love but to be love itself – for what else can love be now, but painful memories?

But painful or not he has the unrealistic desire to preserve those memories forever. The images that come to his mind are of a bridge across a river and – yes – a white spire in the sky. He recognises these ideas as clichés; but maybe they provide some kind of counterbalance against those other clichés, those of rain and barren earth. He will try and remember. He is crying, he isn't sure why.

He looks at Lizzie, the ghost, whatever it is, and she is still smiling at him. He smiles back sadly.

'You always were the bright one,' he says.

There is no reply.

'I am right; life is pointless,' he says, smiling. She always managed to make him see how hollow his arguments were. Intellectually justifiable, but hollow. Her smile is sad too, he realises. He closes his eyes because the sight of her hurts too much. How can she be dead? He can't imagine how she could ever fade.

When he opens his eyes the ghost is gone. He turns around but can't see anyone, only the squirrel cautiously reappearing into the quiet.

\*     \*     \*

Three months pass, in a blur.

He still grieves, still sometimes feels desolate and furious inside. But such moments grow less and less frequent. He keeps his house in order, having filled in all the cracks. He does his job well but not excessively so. He makes mistakes, the worst being to take Marie out on a date during which he just talks about Lizzie. He said sorry to her with a bunch of flowers. He is content for a while not to have a real social life, just occasional pints with Peter who understands he may not want to talk at all.

He is a quieter man than before, and his movements are slower.

Of course his memories fade, are eroded. This makes him uneasy sometimes. He sits in their house, which is empty and creaks occasionally like it is still haunted, and wonders why nothing lasts. Even now he broods over the fact that he can't remember what had once happened on that spot in the Oxford park where the ghost had last appeared to him. The location must surely have held some significance for the ghost to appear there – but what? He thinks he and Lizzie had walked there once as students, but he can't remember anything significant occurring. Why had she haunted that spot? If only we could know at the time which moments would be important and could memorise every detail as it happened...

Some nights he sits and broods over thoughts like

these. But most of the time he is con-tent. He goes to Oxford occasionally, on his own, but never takes photographs. Instead he stares at each building, each bridge, each face carved into the old stone, and wonders how he forgot this detail or that one, and vows not to forget this time. He wonders if it was the same for those who built them.

He walks the grounds of the park near Trinity college but nothing returns, nothing that was gone ever comes back to him.

\* \* \*

There was not much to remember.

Just two young people in love, walking through the park one winter, content in each other's presence, not really speaking. He looks up, sees a lone spire above the trees. He briefly realises how happy he is, and wonders whether it will last. Then she says something to him that makes him laugh, and he forgets what he was thinking. Nothing unique or out of the ordinary. Something that happens every day, and is forgotten. Nevertheless, it built their relationship that bit stronger.

The couple walk off, around the park, and on into their lives.

# TRYING TO BE SO QUIET

James Everington

# The Second Wish

James Everington

Despite being fully clothed and on the verge of leaving, Frasier got back into the bed. The sheets were soft and every time he shifted he could smell the familiar scent of his mother's washing powder. Head on the faded pillow, he looked around the familiar room. It was, he guessed, a typical teenager's bedroom, although his mother had attempted to impose order upon it: his books had been placed on the shelves, his C90 tapes were neatly stacked. Faded posters of faded rock stars were half-unpeeled from the walls. A portable TV and an out-of-date games console, both unplugged. And under the single bed a stash of magazines that Frasier's mother would never have approved of. Nor would she approve of this idleness, he thought; she'd call up the stairs telling him to get out of...

A sound downstairs disturbed him. He must have been dozing for his thoughts of just a few second's ago had vanished. What had he been thinking? Had he been listening for something? He thought so, but could no longer remember what for.

Had it been music? This was the house where he had once raided his father's Beatles collection to see if they were all they were cracked up to be, and despite not having listened to them for years he found he still knew the lyrics and melodies more completely than those of other artists he supposedly liked more. He felt disturbed, as though there really was music playing, and he was trying to concentrate on something else. He closed his eyes, stretched out on his teenage bed which was too small for him; the sides pinched at his middle-age spread.

This is, Frasier thought, a pretty odd situation for a forty-two year old man to be in.

There was another sound and he tensed without moving, hushed his breath for fear of making a sound of his own. Was it...? Again, his thoughts were only half-expressed, as part of his mind rebelled at their childishness. Besides, he knew that the sound hadn't been a per-son, in that way you knew the sounds in a house you had lived in for years. Knew its sounds and the sounds of the people who lived there—knew the silences too. The noise had just been the house, probably grouching at his own recent arrival but now settling back into position, like a family pet briefly disturbed. Patch, Frasier thought vaguely. But Patch had been dead for years. The noise had just been the house. Just the house.

From his bed he could see the empty, white-washed sky, prone atop the barren winter fields, where vagrant seagulls moped and pecked. Why were they called seagulls anyway, Frasier thought, when they were fifty miles inland…? It was like the view outside the house was a backdrop that had been created by an inexpert and hurried hand. He knew that the gulls were there every winter, but that didn't make it ring any truer now. Irritably he let his breath out, unaware that he had been holding it. You've got to get up and do something, he told himself, your thoughts are becoming childish and stupid. He looked at the faint vapour of his breath like he'd done as a child, visible because the house was so cold—the central heating now only came on a couple of hours a day. Who had done that, Frasier thought, some hireling of the Lawyer? Did the Lawyer himself have keys? He could have—Frasier had felt too numb when he had gone to see him to remember much that had been said. He saw the Lawyer's long, white, knuckled fingers clutching the familiar keys, the white flesh peeling as if it were really a different colour underneath—maybe the tanned brown of his own. His own hand had seemed too brown and paw-like as he had used the keys to open the front door to the house; he had felt himself an intruder.

The house—again it made a slight sound, one that Frasier couldn't identify as being specifically a floorboard creaking or a window shivering in a draft; a sound he couldn't specifically deny had been someone opening the door to the hall, a footfall on the first step of the stairs. A bare or slippered foot, for his mother had never allowed shoes on in the house. But his thoughts had become ridiculous again, there was of course no one else inside. He shivered with the cold and turned onto his side to see his reflection in the mirror that faced the bed. His reflected body over-ran the mirror on both sides, and the bedroom looked tiny, like he had been crushed into it. This was reinforced by the sloped ceiling—his old bedroom was an attic room built up into the eaves. The new duffle-coat Frasier was wearing looked incongruous with his European tan—Frasier lived and worked on the continent. He had only intended to come back to England for a few days to 'sort things out'—he was an only son so no one else was going to do it. He didn't know why he had come back to the house, there was nothing here he wanted, was there? There would be a house clearance in a couple of days, and then it would be put back on the market. The Lawyer expected it to get almost ten times what his parents had paid for it. They had lived here all their married life.

This noise was loud, sudden, seemingly right in the room, the sound of some creature settling its weight, screeching hideously—he had forgotten how noisy the gulls could sound when they landed on the roof directly above his head. The surprise had given him quite a fright. Irritably Frasier got up from the bed, old routines making sure he ducked his head to avoid banging it on the sloped eaves, unconsciously humming the chorus of an old pop song. He went to the centre of the bedroom where he could stand straight; but he didn't leave the room. Part of him longed to leave—leave his clothes at the hotel, go straight to the airport from here, jet off to blue skies and later sunsets. Yet back in his old room, this perfectly viable option seemed unrealistic, pure escapism. And part of him wished to linger... It was comforting, somehow, to be here, where nothing seemed to have changed. Where he could pre-tend that nothing had changed, despite all that had. Frasier's parents were never coming back.

Obviously.

But...

Frasier's eyes had been unconsciously scanning the bookshelf while his mind had been elsewhere, and had passed over old comic annuals and dinosaur books without comment. But then they had alighted on a miscellany of Macabre Tales For Children! and his thoughts re-adjusted. Why had his mother kept it? (Why keep all this childish stuff?) He remembered being scared stiff by some of the stories in there when he had been young, and even now he hated horror films and novels. He was sure he had thrown the book away long ago. Which story in particular had always kept him awake? The...

The Monkey's Paw. That was it, that old favourite. A story of three wishes, the first seemingly trivial, the second monstrous, the third needed to undo the second... Of course the dead son that the second wish called up was never actually described—the third wish erased him before he could enter the house. And yet as a child Frasier had spent many a sleepless night imagining what the mother would have seen when she flung open the door if that third wish hadn't been granted... Ghost or zombie? Frasier's mind had always tended towards the zombie, something corporeal, something still flesh and blood, with the ruins of dead circuits burnt into the brain, old tics and memories still present deep within the neurones. But... decaying. Clumsy. Quite mad.

Stop it. Stop it, Frasier told himself. Why are you thinking like this? He hadn't thought of the tale of The Monkey's Paw in years. He supposed it was being back in his old room, his old house, that had done it.

The seagull on the roof, sounding about three times its real size, shifted its weight above

Frasier's head. The sounds of its ponderous movements echoed into the interior of the house, and died. Frasier paused, as if something else might answer them.

But of course, Frasier thought, I have been back here before, many times. Every Christmas for a start. He had always enjoyed returning to his parent's house at Christmas (he had no family save them). It had seemed an abdication of responsibility, somehow, to return. He had nothing to do with the organisation of Christmas Day, and his parents' routine hadn't changed in twenty-five years: get up and open presents, get driven to the pub by his Mum (who would have a bitter-shandy), let his Dad buy the first round, and he would buy the second; home to sit in the living room pretending to watch TV but really dozing and enjoying the comforting sounds of his mother cooking; and hours later his Dad sharpening the carving knife before the year's biggest dinner… Those three days had been like a bubble separated from the rest of the year, a comfortable regression, like returning to the warmth of your bed after you had already got up once.

He remembered that Doctor—the Lawyer and

the Doctor had looked so much alike that in his grief he had thought them interchangeable, some Pantomime mastermind swapping coats, donning a false moustache and reappearing. He had asked the Lawyer complex medical questions, and tried to entrust to the Doctor all of the estate's legal affairs. He remembered how the Lawyer's paid-by-the-hour professionalism had flickered for a second, behind his costume-shop glasses. The Lawyer's long, white, doctor's fingers had calmly closed the open file on his desk, and the man had stood up and briskly urged Frasier to get a hold of himself. Although the estate was small the tax situation was complicated and required Frasier's full attention...

He sat back on his bed again, the copy of Macabre Tales clutched in his hands. But he wasn't thinking of that. What was he thinking of? That damn Lawyer? But he had wanted to think about the Doctor... Not wanted to exactly, but... A noise briefly disturbed him. Frasier's thoughts struggled closer to the surface, to the source of the noise; then retreated.

The Doctor had been a thin, unhealthy figure, dressed in a shiny white coat that looked too big for him, looked brand new. Frasier had been breathing heavily—ever since he'd woken up in the unfamiliar hotel room he had been hyperventilating and fighting the urge to flee. If he wasn't here then it wouldn't be happening. The Doctor had slowly pulled off his clear plastic gloves with a snapping sound, and again Frasier thought things couldn't possibly be real—oh, he knew doctors wore gloves, but in their office? The details didn't seem right. Without asking he went over to the window to get some fresh air. He peered down from the tenth floor. Incorrectly sized people all ceased staring up towards him and pretended to go about their business... Get a grip, Frasier told himself; but the problem was that he didn't want to get a grip because then he would have to deal with the situation. But maybe he would have to anyway, for the Doctor was talking and the sound jarred his thoughts.

'... not unusual. Of course it's easy to see why it might seem a staggering coincidence to you, almost macabre, but when a husband and a wife have been married that long... well, it's not unusual if one passes away for the other to become sick relatively quickly afterwards. Of course the speed of your father's decline in this case is almost exceptional—there must have been undetected symptoms for a while—but I think it's safe to say that the psychological shock contributed...'

'I couldn't even fly back in time!' Frasier shouted, turning away from the open window. The sounds coming from it seemed cliché too, a backing-tape of car horns, gull calls, a workman's drill, and kids shrieking. 'I heard about... mother, and I... true, I had to sort some of my business affairs out but... I got a flight as soon as I could after, and by the time I'd landed, he...' The anger didn't feel good; but it purged other feelings that were worse. When did I last see my parents? Frasier thought. Last Christmas—they'd been disappointed that he had come alone, again. He took another of his shallow, labour-intensive gulps of air, and tried to stop the room spinning by focusing on that point and that point, connecting them with a straight mental line. The cheap white walls of the Doctor's office seemed to move and shake, as if they were propped up from behind with wooden slats. He realised the Doctor was speaking again.

The Doctor spoke slowly, like one unused to being interrupted, to improvisation. He explained that while the speed in the cases of his parents was remarkable, the circumstances themselves weren't. He's saying all the same things again! Frasier thought, with a touch of hysteria. His thoughts felt as fast and shallow as his breathing. The Doctor's voice sped up again as he regained his confidence and professional demeanour; Frasier stopped listening to the words. He stared at the Doctor, convinced that the man wasn't blinking… Of course he knew this thought was ridiculous and lacked significance even if it was true. Yet—he wasn't blinking! His mind fought for some sense of what was going on, some connection to make things manageable.

A sound downstairs—Frasier sat up slowly, blinking as his thoughts returned to where he was. He had got back into bed without even realising. Actually in it this time, curled up beneath the covers. His body felt warm and groggy, as if he had been asleep, but he knew that was impossible (he had barely slept at all, these last few days). But just what noise downstairs had disturbed him? There could be no one else in the house but him. And he didn't even know what he was doing there—he had intended to go back home as soon as possible. But that word rang funny in his head—he couldn't connect 'home' with that sprawling white house on the Med, with its balcony overlooking the port, its sun-trap patio, the backroom he had converted into a home-office, complete with technology that would have seemed fiction to him twenty years ago. And his bedroom, where he slept alone: cool bare walls, a cool tiled floor, open, spacious, quiet, all that he could wish for. How had he ended up there, how could he afford it? His career, his life since leaving home seemed some-what fantastical, a tenuous series of events that lacked coherence or any verisimilitude.

He couldn't connect this house to that house, and sitting up dozily in his teenage bed it was as if everything after the age of eighteen had been one of those dreams that seemed reasonable enough while sleeping, but preposterous upon waking. Christ, Frasier thought, how would I have coped if they'd both died while I'd been living at home? At the thought, his hurt found new nerves, when he'd thought all inside was dead. There was no sense to be made of it—at the back of all his adult thoughts there seemed to be a child's voice, persistent, praying.

Still, what had been moving downstairs? But no, Frasier told himself, it's just the house playing tricks on you. You knew the sounds in your own house—and he had known that sound. The house had tics and strange coughs, the same as people did. He remembered the strange, high-pitched cough of his father, up early on Christmas morning, and how he had been able to hear it through his bedroom wall as he had stayed in bed...

Frasier got up—it was time to leave. It was too cold in this stupid house, in this stupid country—he had his work to get back to, his sunny terrace, and the sounds of real seagulls, following the sardine boats out to sea... Back to a foreign tongue and being alone, Frasier thought, that's waiting for me too: waking up in an unfamiliar bedroom that you've slept in for so many years, with the hot night seeming to crackle with sounds on the edge of hearing. But he would get over things, Frasier told himself. Hadn't he read that the death of one's parents could be the opportunity for psychological and philosophical growth? Because accepting their death meant accepting yours—there was no one between you and the grave now. He knew that to be true, and the idea sat neat and pat in his thoughts. Too neat—the concept seemed tightly wrapped and didn't connect with anything else. It seemed to have as much relevance to real life as a Christmas cracker motto.

Like they were eager for the chance, his thoughts turned to Christmases past. He sat back on the bed again.

And lay down beneath the covers.

There was the sound of more birds settling on the roof, and a second sound that Frasier took no notice of.

His mind seemed to be turning over his childhood thoughts, recasting them in the language of middle-age, as if his whole life had been merely a process to allow him to complete thoughts and idles he had started years ago. He remembered lying in this very bed, unable to sleep because of the images the book of Macabre Tales put into his mind—images that changed every random sound that the house made into something purposeful and malignant.

The monkey's paw itself, Frasier thought, is just a prop, it's just a hook for the author to hang his hat on—it isn't necessary to the story, it isn't the cause of what happens. Not really, not what drives it underneath. It was the wishes, the built up prayers and frustrations of the characters

being condensed into one moment's speech…
Belief wasn't even needed; who'd believe in the
stupid story of The Monkey's Paw? It was just the
wanting that was important. Frasier curled
himself up under the covers, screwed shut his
eyes like a child pretending to sleep.

When he had signed the documents the
Lawyer had presented to him Frasier had felt
happier, because it clearly hadn't been his
signature on the forms. The handwriting had
been neat, business-like, almost boasting with its
unnecessary loops and flourishes. He
remembered practicing his signature when he'd
first been old enough to need one, and it had
taken many attempts for his childish and
freewheeling handwriting to settle into anything
adult and consistent. And now the signature that
he'd just signed didn't look like his at all, and so it
couldn't have been him who'd signed away his
parent's house into the hands of this stranger…
Frasier put the lid back on the pen and handed it
and the documents back to the Lawyer. Frasier
looked at the certificates and leather-bound books
behind the man—like a film set I saw somewhere,
he thought. He wanted to flee, but to where? The
hotel he was staying in seemed unreal, a stage

mid-production; the staff treated him like he was someone else.

He heard a sound. It was his own name. The Lawyer was speaking. He was telling Frasier that there was no need to linger in the country. That he was no doubt anxious to be back home. Frasier was watching the man's hands.

The Lawyer's hands were making spasmodic, grasping motions inside his rubber gloves... But no—Frasier shook his head as if to dislodge the random connections. Then he stared at the Lawyer's long, white, latex-looking fingers as they grasped at the air.

'Huh?' he said, aware that he had missed something.

'I said, any remaining items of personal value will need to be retrieved before the house clearance...' Personal value—there was something horribly adult about those words, that didn't fit with the child-like wishes he was making between breathes, almost between thoughts. Still, that was how he had ended up coming back to the house one last time.

It sounded like someone's footstep on the bottom stair. A soft but clumsy sound, not of something unused to its surroundings, but unused to its own movements...—two such things, Frasier thought, for there was a repetition that wasn't an echo. Stop making such imaginative connections, he told himself, foetal beneath the blankets.

Frasier hadn't realised that the death of his parents would affect him to such a degree. After all, he had been independent for years now hadn't he? He'd seen them at most twice a year. And the memories he had of them—his Dad's Sixties vinyl, his Mum's Christmas cooking—these seemed slight things he had dredged up in order to justify his hurt. The hurt—the hurt he had expected. What had been surprising had been the sense of cords cut, of loss—the loss of a sensible and consistent world. The world Frasier had inhabited in the days since: the villa with the picture-postcard views, the nowhere land of the airport and the blank view from the plane that could have been flying anywhere, the cold and misty country of his birth, the hotel room he could barely remember seconds after turning the lights out—all of this seemed unrealistic somehow, a film set cluttered yet insubstantial, nothing that could explain or even contain the fact of his parents being dead. It had hurt

Frasier's eyes to look at and he had kept blinking, braced for it all to collapse and cohere into something more meaningful—something more awful certainly, but at least more meaningful—more in tune with his thoughts. But the paper-thin world had remained standing, and he had recoiled into nostalgia and solipsism.

You can't be mad, Frasier thought, because if you doubt your own mind then that proves you're thinking right. That was what people said.

He could hear the sounds clearly now, despite the fact that his head was under the covers; something seemed to stumble as it climbed the stairs, and it threw out an arm to sup-port itself—Frasier could picture it. This time, the sounds didn't fade as he concentrated on them.

The feeling of insubstantiality and fakery had left as soon as he had entered his old house. It was like the decades had fallen away—the stage-sets and bit-part players revealed for what they were. He had thought it all dream-like even as he had dreamt it...—now the only evidence he seemed to have that he was an adult were the clothes he was wearing. Irritably, Frasier got out of bed and looked at himself in the mirror. The duffel-coat looked both childish and too big.

You'll grow into it, he remembered his mother saying.

Inches from his head, on the other side of the sloping roof, there was the clamour and clattering sound of the seagulls taking off all at the same time, as if something had spooked them. Frasier watched them from the window, some calling raucously, some heads down and determined to be away. The sounds of the footsteps were wrong, limping and out of synch. But they were right too, for he felt he recognised them. The sounds of your own home were always recognisable. Frasier could hear it was a struggle for them to climb the staircase, but heard no muffled curses, no heavy breathing. Just the slow and patient footsteps. But Frasier wasn't worried; his mind had dulled, all his feelings had calmed. Absently, he let the book of Macabre Tales fall open—but it had always fallen open at that place, where there was a deep grove in the spine. He didn't have to read it, the smell of the old, open book seemed to bring the story back entire: Without was a cold and desolate night where a man could barely see his hand in front of his face; but within the small parlour of the house the shutters were drawn and the fire burned brightly… This house, Frasier thought, has always been a place where I have abdicated responsibility for my actions. Of course he was being ridiculous, there were no footsteps three-quarters of the way up the stairs. It was just the house. But, his childhood voice told him, it wasn't the believing that mattered, it was the wanting.

Why was he getting rid of the house? That thought rocked Frasier's eyes open, like the first sad thought upon awakening. He had signed it all over to that grasping Lawyer. Why had he done that? He didn't need the money straight away, not with his dream-job… His parents, if they had known, would have been angry and wanting to punish him. But no, they had never punished him. Did he want to punish himself?

The sounds were near the top of the stairs now, and Frasier realised a different reason why he might find them familiar—because he might have imagined them so many times in the night when he had been unable to sleep, when his mind had fixated on the dreadful and vengeful thing that the second wish had called up: the clutching, bare white fingers, the grin of the mad skull visible through the pallid adult face; the shambling, uncoordinated footsteps that would have seemed hesitant if it wasn't for the slow but unstoppable insistence of its limp…

What else could his mind have dredged up but what was already there?

The book fell from his hands with a clatter that seemed to break his stupor. The window in his attic bedroom was too small and acutely angled; the only escape was to leave the room and run across the landing of the stairs quickly before they got to the top, then into the bathroom where there was a large window that always rattled in the wind…

But still, Frasier thought as he opened the door (he couldn't see what was coming up the stairs; they hadn't reached the top yet) what am I escaping to? Nothing that seemed real. And didn't he have the memories of his parents in his mind too? If it's really a case of wanting and not believing, Frasier thought, then wouldn't I have used my final wish to stop all this happening, if that is what I wanted?

Even as he ran from his bedroom, he wasn't sure if it was to escape the sounds he heard coming up the stairs, or if he was rushing to meet them.

# THE SECOND WISH

# Damage

On the second day of Christmas, Alex's true love died. A year later, she tried to follow her.

It seemed appropriate to end things in the room she most associated with Alyssa: they had called it 'the snug', a small, cosy room situated at the back of the house. It was a room that seemed older than the rest of the house, with wooden floorboards and exposed ceiling beams, a real fireplace streaked with soot, Alyssa's faded paperback poetry books and wild-life guides. And a view of the garden—Alex remembered how, whenever Alyssa had entered the snug, she'd always looked outside before sitting down, to see what birds were in the gar-den. Alex had never shown an interest when Alyssa was alive, but now she recalled the things her lover had tried to show her: the stop-start movement of blackbirds, the clattering, dramatic escapes of wood pigeons, the alert poise of magpies. On this second day of Christ-mas, though, the garden was devoid of life or movement, stripped back and de-coloured by winter.

And no doves. Never any doves, since that day.

'It's a stupid song,' she remembered Alyssa saying. 'Turtle doves migrate during the winter— that's partly why their numbers are declining, they get shot over Spain—so why are they in a Christmas song?'

The memory seemed so bright and overpowering, the hurt of it so enduring, that it was odd to realise that, in a few minutes, it would be dead along with Alex herself. She used that realisation to ward off the hurt, one last time. Not that the pain of Alyssa's death was something that came and went; it was damage permanently done.

So:

Alex turned away from the window and moved

a small wooden chair into the centre of the room, beneath the beam from which she'd already secured the scarf, tied into a noose at the other end. Surprising herself she shivered; no fire had been lit in the fireplace since the last one had burnt out a year ago.

'Turtle doves pair for life,' she remembered Alyssa saying, when she'd seen two of them in the garden. Alex climbed onto the chair and put the noose around her neck, the first time she'd allowed the soft material of the scarf to touch her skin.

The room has always been Alyssa's space more than hers; now it made sounds as if it too were hurting, the groans and creaks of something old. Alex absently wondered who the first person to step inside here after she was dead would be.

She paused once, as if listening for a sound that wasn't there, then stepped from the chair and kicked it over. The clearness of her vision fluttered away, her sight smoked over.

She'd been expecting the pain of course, hoped the vodka and tablets she'd taken would at least lessen what she anticipated as a ring of hurt around her neck, a dreadful straining in her lungs. What she hadn't expected was the burning sensation instant across her entire body, like her nerves were being seared. Even as her hands automatically plucked at the scarf around her neck, she tried to look with dimming eyes for a source of heat—a pyre so blazing must surely be visible. As if she were being burnt alive for the crime of loving Alyssa, or of outliving her. But whatever the source of the pain she was prepared to follow it down where it led, prepared to let it pull her away and overwhelm her... Numb fingers slipped from the scarf, her legs ceased to flail so vigorously scant inches from the floor...

And then it was as if there was something soft yet heavy beating the air around her, a purring, throaty sound like trickling water... Something seemed to lift her, slip the noose from her neck, and lower her attentively to the ground.

Trembling legs collapsed beneath her; she was left breathing deep, wretched gulps of air from the cold and lonely world, an unwanted present reluctantly taken. Her head sank to the floor, her blurred vision gradually focussed on the movement of year old ash in the fire-place, disturbed by her presence. The sounds of the house continued around her, like some-thing flickering from room to room.

\*　　\*　　\*

Alyssa had been hit by a car, driven by a flustered old man in a flap about the new one-way system, slamming the accelerator not the brake. The Alzheimers searing his brain leaving him incapable of standing trial, in care and insensible before the inquest had even taken place. No one to blame, no one to be angry with.

Alyssa had only been present because she'd been looking for an extra gift for Alex in the Boxing Day sales. And she'd found one; the police had handed Alex a bag when they'd arrived to break the news. Inside, a man's scarf, which Alex knew Alyssa would have picked to remind her of her favourite TV show. Her girlfriend had sat and watched the Doctor Who Christmas special with the same affectionate bafflement Alex had felt when Alyssa had called her to see a bird in the garden.

The long, striped scarf had reminded her of a noose even then.

Until she tried to kill herself, Alex hadn't taken the scarf out of its bag. Knew it would hurt too much, and she'd spent a year unsuccessfully trying to avoid those things which would hurt too much: speaking to Alyssa's family or their old friends, going to see the place where she'd died. She hadn't watched the Christmas special this year. Too much potential for damage.

And today she had wanted the hurt to end. But it hadn't.

Alex turned over on the floor of the snug, looked up. The top of the scarf was still tied to the black wooden beam above; its neck was still noosed. The chair had toppled over, well away from her swinging feet. How had she survived? Somehow slipped from the noose? But its grip had been firm around her neck; she could feel its phantom pressure even now. And besides, it hadn't felt like she'd just fell. It had felt like someone, something, had lifted her to stop her choking before placing her with gentle, hideous cruelty back into the world.

Alex looked at the scarf, the toppled chair, knew she wouldn't be able to try again, and wept onto the wooden floorboards.

*   *   *

Later, she stared out into the empty garden, her

entire body devoid of feeling. It was a dull, grey winter day outside, of the kind no one wanted but everyone had caused: it so rarely snowed, anymore, it being hotter. Climate change being another thing Alyssa said had caused the decline of turtle doves. Alex remembered her lover's face when the pair of birds had come to nest in their garden, a small, joyful memory swinging loose and destructive in-side of her. Inner pain surged but had nowhere to go; her outer self remained numb. It was starting to get cold in their—her—house and Alex welcomed the thought of shivering, of a cold harsh enough to touch her nerves. But then she heard the click of the boiler's timer, and even that was denied to her.

She had taken down the scarf and was letting it slide through her fingers, end on end, and couldn't feel its touch. She stopped, briefly raised a hand to her neck. She could feel the bruised skin there, it should surely be tender to the touch, burning even with the sting of the air—but it didn't hurt at all.

For a moment, Alex doubted if she'd even gone through with the attempt.

Later still, she went to the kitchen, put a pan of water on to boil, stuck in some spaghetti she knew she'd never eat. The pan was too small and the end of the spaghetti stuck out from the top; Alex reached to push it down into the bubbling water. She imagined her self screaming aloud, pushing her hand further down, into the seething heat itself, so that then she'd at least feel something: a hot and terrible pain nevertheless on the outside of her, not touching her core like the grief of Alyssa's passing. And then she was surprised to see that she hadn't just pictured it, her hand was in the boiling water. She stared at it blankly, as if it weren't part of her at all, refraction seeming to confirm the illusion. Her vision blurred at the edges as if flames were flickering just out of sight, bird-like cinders wheeling away. Then Alex pulled her hand out of the bubbling, surging water, saw how red and inflamed it was.

She hadn't felt anything at all.

\*　　\*　　\*

Punching the wall, using nail-clippers on the flesh of her foot, jabbing the point of a knife into the skin between thumb and finger—Alex soon found it was true: she could no longer feel any physical pain. She saw the blood rise, the bruises swell, but felt nothing. No sensation. Yet each time she damaged herself her vision scorched over, birds of muted flame flickering briefly to life before burning out. They made noises like embers dying, like logs un-der the chimney shifting and collapsing as they cooled.

It was as if a hard, unfeeling carapace had grown over her naked soul, pointless protection over something already broken. Alex tried to think, clearly, about suicide, but was dismayed to find that despite her grief the thought of knotting that scarf again, of kicking away that chair again, was still too much. To try again, to fail again, fall again back into the hurting world, staring into the empty echo of a cold fireplace... Had her attempt been nothing but a cry for help? But a cry to whom—she knew no one was listening.

Her best hope was that given her new inability to feel physical hurt, she would accidentally injure herself to a degree that might prove fatal.

\*    \*    \*

Alex wasn't sure why, but almost a year to the day since Alyssa's death she decided to finally see the place where it had happened. As if the lack of sensation outside was a goad to heighten the pain inside. She knew seeing the place would hurt like hell, and her thoughts pulled away from the idea in the same way her hand should have reacted to the boiling water... yet still, she went.

She was a sight, she knew, her face and forearms patterned with cuts and bruises, her hair unwashed, clothes unmatched, and her right hand hanging from her arm, unbandaged and livid red. People stared at her, some called out in concern or mockery, but she was hardened against any feeling of embarrassment.

There was nothing significant about the spot where Alyssa had died, an ordinary section of pavement outside a shop selling quarter-price Christmas cards and tinsel. Two pigeons, dirty and mad-eyed, pecking at something someone had dropped. They had green and white marks around their necks, Alex noticed, like bruises, like blisters. She looked at her hands again, to confirm the reality of the hurt she should be feeling, but wasn't. When she looked back up, a group of youths smoking weed pushed past her, one of them idly kicking one of the pigeons as they did so.

It was the idleness that did it, Alex later

reflected, the sheer casualness of the hurt.

The pigeon lurched wide-eyed away from the blow; it seemed to be crippled in one wing and despite flapping didn't take flight. Alex knew she would barely have noticed the mangy thing's pain, before, nor the way its companion paused in its eating. But Alyssa would have, she knew; Alyssa had always felt things too much.

Alex looked again at her seared and blistered hand, numb and hanging heavy from her arm. Before she could second guess herself she followed the boys as they turned off the main street, down a path that led to a boarded up church. Looking for somewhere to smoke their weed out of sight. The three lads opened the gate to the churchyard, went inside and sat near some of the older trees with boughs like gallows. Alex followed them. One of them looked up.

'Hellooooo gorgeous!' the boy crowed; the others jeered. As Alex approached she saw they were much closer to her own age than she'd thought. Laid off in the recent factory cuts, she supposed. Smoking to dull their pained astonishment at being on the scrapheap so young. Why the hell not, Alyssa would have said. She would have sympathised. But Alex had so little room inside of her for other emotions, now.

The boy stood as she approached, a grin on his lips. Alex stretched her mouth into an answering smile she couldn't feel at all. She stopped a pace or two from the boy, wondering if she was really going to do this, wondering if this was the one who had kicked the pigeon, wondering if she cared.

'Hey, sit down beautiful, sit down with us...' the boy leered and moved to touch her hip. His movements faltered as he saw her red right hand, which clenched...

Alex found it surprisingly easy to punch someone when you couldn't feel pain in your fist. As if she were disconnected from the results. At the sound of the blow, birds she hadn't previously noticed in the long grass blurred upwards in the corners of her vision, the colour of cinnamon and ash.

The boy's head was knocked back; he cried aloud and clutched a hand to his nose, blood seeping through his fingers. He stared at Alex in shock. She hit him again, saw the birds fly, and the boy reeled away shouting incoherently. The others took one look at her and bolted; the boy she had hit stumbled after them. She had to restrain herself not to follow, had to force her first to unclench.

As she walked away she tried hard not to think what Alyssa would have thought about it, had she been present. The boys had deserved it, after all.

And for a moment—just a brief numb moment—had it been enough?

\*   \*   \*

December 27th

Police are investigating reports of an incident outside The Partridge & Pear public house on Glassworks Street. Witnesses say that a man, in his late 30s, left the pub after being belligerent to staff and customers and was then physically assaulted by a woman who had followed him outside. Both parties fled the scene rather than wait for medical attention; it was claimed that the assailant had looked injured prior to the altercation with the victim, but whether this was the motive for the attack is unclear. Police are appealing for both parties to come forward.

\*   \*   \*

December 29th

A 65 year old lady was attacked outside the Jehovah's Witness Kingdom Hall in the town centre last night. The victim, identified as Mary Baker, was left semi-concussed and needed stitches to her face and arms after the attack, which the police described as 'unfeeling'. The attacker was described as female, young, slim, with a bruised and bloodied face. Robbery has been excluded as a motive, as the victim's gold rings were not taken from her fingers, or her purse or phone. Mrs Baker has been prominent in the local media recently with her condemnations of what she described as the 'sickness' of the LGBT community, but the possibility this was a revenge attack remains speculation. Police are appealing for witnesses.

\*     \*     \*

December 30th

A police spokesperson has expressed mounting concern about the spate of vicious assaults in the town, after a series of unsolved attacks over the last week. Victims describe a young woman, looking in need of medical attention, but ferocious in her attacks and unable to be subdued. Victims appear to have been targeted either for violent behaviour in the streets or for being supporters of politically conservative, far-right or discriminatory groups. The latest known victim was Carlton Foster, 29, recently convicted of animal cruelty for throwing darts at geese and ducks on the canal. Police are appealing for calm and witnesses.

\*    \*    \*

It wasn't enough.

Alex couldn't make sense of who she was supposed to be anymore. If she caught a glimpse of herself in a mirror or shop window then what she saw—bloodied and cracked lips; new bruises over old; swollen, blackened flesh beneath her eyes—was a person who should be hurting. She should sense, surely, those scratches to her face, the bruised and split knuckles, the empty socket where a tooth had been? But there was nothing, as if the reflection wasn't her. She turned her head to watch it even as she walked away, seeing but not feeling its limping, crooked gait.

She still felt grief hanging heavy and heart-wrenching within, of course; hurting those people hadn't assuaged that. Maybe because it hadn't felt like her doing it. Hadn't felt like she had really hurt them; hadn't felt like anything at all. If they could be hurt, that was. She didn't know, anymore. What if they felt as little as she did? What if their nerves were seared numb too?

Thinking such thoughts, Alex sat alone in the snug hearing the sounds of the house flutter around her, looking out into the motionless colours of the garden or towards the dull ashes of the fireplace. The scarf was still hung from its beam, there seemed little point in taking it down. Or had she retied it? Alex wasn't sure. The chair was upright in position under the noosed scarf too, so she must have picked that up from where it had fallen.

As she sat, she invariably picked and pinched at her fingers until they bleed around the nails, or stuck a pin in them, or slapped her face. She saw embers flying in the shapes of birds every time she damaged herself, heard the crackling of something burning. As if her body had to find some way of letting her know about pain, even though she could no longer sense it. Or as if the house or something within it were trying to tell her, an external nervous system of sight and sound, with its heart in the snug. In there, Alex heard flames beat and lap as if the fireplace was in use, saw in the sides of her vision the downbeat of soft wings, cinnamon and mottled black...

...she was digging a pin again and again into the flesh of her arm, as if the colours and sounds weren't distractions from her self-harming but...

'Turtle doves mate for life,' she remembered Alyssa saying. 'In some poems, it's the Phoenix they mate with. Shakespeare.'

The Phoenix! Alex thought with forced scorn, trying to drown out the memory. Re-born from fire! She thought of her own rebirth, pissing herself as she hung from a Doctor Who scarf, burnt until her ashy remains were pulled down, dragged by cruel forceps into a painful and unwanted second life...

...digging into her flesh again and again as if the colours and sounds weren't a dis-traction, but the harm a distraction from the sounds of birds and phantom flames...

And then she realised:

The din of invisible fire and flapping wings seemed to shrink and concatenate to a point as sharp as the pinprick.

What she'd been hearing wasn't all around the house, but echoing from a specific place. Something was trapped in the chimney.

Alex stood, then walked towards the stained fireplace (moving aside the mysteriously righted wooden chair as she did so). She knelt down by it, hearing the sounds of something struggling, frantic, fading, coming from the open mouth of the chimney. It sounded close, near the bottom. What should she do?

She thought, briefly, of lighting a fire beneath—it was cold enough to feel justified, and the simplest way to solve the problem. Burn the fucking noisy thing. But she knew that the memory of Alyssa wouldn't allow her to do that, and after all, didn't it deserve to be pulled down into hateful life again as she had? Its sounds continued, stronger as if it sensed her presence on the other side of its brick prison and wasn't sure if she were friend or foe. With shaking hands, Alex took out her phone and looked up how to rescue birds stuck in chimneys. She had to wipe smears of her blood off the phone screen by the time she was done.

Alex fetched a torch and the scarf with which she'd tried to kill herself—but hadn't it been retied to the beam, she thought?—which she now wrapped around one hand to protect it. Looking up, she confirmed her suspicions about the bird's location: there was a small stone lip a few feet up the chimney and something was perched on it. She saw the pinprick gleam of maddened eyes, the shadows of bent wings trying to find space to flap. She reached up with her covered hand; there was a tremendous clattering and soot fell down, making her nose itch, but she succeeded in grabbing the flailing thing. Gingerly she pulled it down de-spite its struggles to escape her grasp and die. When she took it out from the chimney she could see from the cinder colours of its head that it was a turtle dove.

But how could that be? Turtle doves migrated during the winter—Alyssa had said so. At the memory, she had to stop her hands from tightly squeezing that which they held. She moved towards the door which opened out onto the garden—in the glass her reflection looked as crazed and soot-streaked as the dove itself. She cursed herself for not opening the door first, now she had to struggle to open it with the bird in her hands. Her efforts caused the scarf to partially unwrap from her hands; the dove's legs were freed and it raked its surprisingly sharp claws across her exposed wrists.

Alex gasped in pain, and then gasped in surprise: she had felt it. Felt the hurt of the damage done to her. It had been so long since she'd felt physical hurt it was like a new experience, almost pleasurable. The pain burnt.

She fumbled at the door again, her head rushing with the sounds of flame, of beating wings, of Alyssa's voice. The turtle dove scratched at her again, pecked her tender flesh. Alex managed to get the door open, threw her bloody hands up and let go, saw the flash of cinnamon breast and dappled wings, then cursed as the dove circled, flew back into the room. Into Alyssa's room. There was no sense of panic to it now she had released it, but a feeling of grace. It curved past the fireplace, over the comfy sofa and wooden chair, past the shelves of Alyssa's books.

Following it into the centre of the room, wondering what to do now, Alex rubbed at the pain in her wrist. As she did so, she felt all her other self-inflicted wounds come alive with delayed hurt, a hundred minute damages at once. Like fire. Phoenix & The Turtle, she remembered a sweet voice saying. The dove flapped too close to her, too close to focus, so that it seemed to grow, become blurred in her vision, aflame... Then it was gone from the room, streaking out into the garden and away. Alex collapsed onto the floor, the scarf running through her hands, knocking the wooden chair over as she did so...

\*    \*    \*

She stood up on trembling legs, unsure if time had passed since she'd fallen or not. Her head was ringing with strange, fading sounds of birds; she couldn't remember fully what had happened. Every part of her hurt. But alive, she was alive.

There was a scarf on the floor, a tipped over wooden chair. She realised the door to the garden was open; had she opened it? Cold Christmas air streamed through it; the old, pre-global warming cold, for once. Might it even snow?

Alex saw movement in the garden as she shut the door; saw a bird Alyssa would no doubt have watched avidly.

Alex stood watching the bird for a few minutes herself, the orange of its presence in the bare black boughs of the trees somehow unworldly. Then it flew off. Alex, almost with-out thinking, took one of Alyssa's books from the shelves; a bird guide so she could identify what it has been. The book fell open at the right page—turtle dove—because there was a bookmark there, as if that were the last bird Alyssa had looked at. As her body ached, Alex pictured her dead lover's face. The hurt inside her at the memory was as sweet as bird song...

It was the second day of Christmas.

# DAMAGE

Trying To Be So Quiet was originally published
by Boo Books (2016)

The Second Wish first appeared in a different
version in Supernatural Tales #23 (2013)

Damage first appeared in 12 Darks Days: One
Hell Of A Christmas, Nocturnicorn Press (2017)

# ABOUT THE AUTHOR

**James Everington** mainly writes dark, supernatural fiction, although he occasionally takes a break and writes dark, non-supernatural fiction. His second collection of such tales, Falling Over, is out now from Infinity Plus.

He's also the author of The Quarantined City, an episodic novel mixing Borgesian strangeness with supernatural horror—'an unsettling voice all of its own' The Guardian—and the novellas Paupers' Graves and The Shelter.

Alongside Dan Howarth, he has co-edited the anthologies The Hyde Hotel (Black Shuck Books) and the BFS Award nominated Imposter Syndrome (Dark Minds Press).

Oh, and he drinks Guinness, if anyone's asking. You can find out what James is currently up to at his *Scattershot Writing* site.

jameseverington.blogspot.com

# THE BLACK ROOM
MANUSCRIPTS VOLUME
FOUR

James Everington features in *The Black Room Manuscripts Volume Four* with his short story **Size Isn't Everything.**

# THE BLACK ROOM MANUSCRIPTS VOLUME FOUR

SINISTER
HORROR
COMPANY

Some words are born in shadows.

Some tales told only in whispers.

Under the paper thin veneer of our sanity is a world
that exists. Hidden just beyond, in plain sight,
waiting to consume you should you dare stray from
the street-lit paths that sedate our fears.
For centuries the Black Room has stored stories
of these encounters, suppressing the knowledge of
the rarely seen. Protecting the civilised world from
its own dark realities.
The door to the Black Room has once again
swung open to unleash twenty five masterful tales
of the macabre from the twisted minds of a new
breed of horror author.

The Black Room holds many secrets.

Dare you enter…one final time?

*Other books by James Everington*

**Novels & Novellas:**
Paupers' Graves, Hersham Horror (2016)
The Quarantined City, Infinity Plus (2016)
The Shelter (2011)

**Short Story Collections:**
Imposter Syndrome (Editor), Dark Minds Press (2017)
The Hyde Hotel (Editor), Black Shuck Books (2016)
Falling Over, Infinity Plus (2013)
The Other Room (2011)

The Sinister Horror Company is an independent UK publisher of genre fiction. Their mission a simple one – to write, publish and launch innovative and exciting genre fiction by themselves and others.

For further information on the Sinister Horror Company visit:

SinisterHorrorCompany.com
Facebook.com/sinisterhorrorcompany
Twitter @SinisterHC

SINISTERHORRORCOMPANY.COM